This book belongs to

This book is dedicated to my very
own Fantastic Fin, whom I love dearly!

Acknowledgements

Many thanks to my amazing husband who has supported me all the way, along with my children, family, and dear friends. Special thanks to Sue Miller and Sarah Fountain of TAUK Kids for making my dream a reality. Sincere thanks to *Storytime Magazine*, in particular Lulu, who has helped me to create a wonderful teaching resource pack to go along with this book. Finally, a huge thank you to Andrew Whitehead who has brought this story to life with some awesome illustrations!

Fantastic Fin Faces His Fears

By Jessica Bowers

Illustrated by Andrew Whitehead

First published in 2021 by Jessica Bowers Well-being Writer

ISBN 978-1-5272-9886-6

TAUK Kids

Children's Book Publishers
A Division of Team Author UK

JESSICA
BOWERS
WELL-BEING WRITER

Written by
Jessica Bowers

FANTASTIC FIN
FACES HIS FEARS
BOOK 1

Illustrated by Andrew Whitehead

Fantastic Fin is **brave** today,
but he wasn't always this way.
Always **fantastic**, this is true,
his braveness was a seed that grew.

The stories that are written here,
shows just how Fin did face his fears.

Fantastic Fin was **feeling fear,**
the rugby game was drawing near.
Inside him he was feeling **dread,**
he wished he could go home instead.

Then he thought of
something **cool,**
his **mind** could be a
useful tool.

Fantastic Fin
wanted to cry,
he stood alone
and felt so shy.

His friend was poorly and went home;
he felt quite bored there on his own.

He turned into a **super spy**,
and watched the children play nearby.
He spied a boy stood on his own,
looking **sad** and **all alone**.

To the boy,
Fin did **bravely** say,
"Would you like to come
and **play**?"

The spy and boy did exchange names
and played a really **fun-filled game**.
Fantastic Fin the super spy, overcame
his feeling **shy**.

Fantastic Fin **played** with some toys,
with other **girls** and other **boys**.

Then came a boy who did **not** share,
he scowled and growled and caused a scare.
Fin and his friends felt some **worry**,
unsure how to sort the **bully**.

Then he **thought** of something cool,
his **mind** could be a useful tool.
Fantastic Fin became a **knight**,
his armour **saved him** from his fright.

Fantastic Fin said, "**Come and play,**
but **share** and do watch what you say!"

Fantastic Fin became a knight
and **saved the day** to all's delight.

Fantastic Fin felt dull and drab,
at school he had to have his jab.

He didn't want the painful prick,
the **thought** of it made him
feel sick.

Then he thought of **something cool**,
his **mind** could be a useful tool.
Fin's mood did soar up from zero,
when **he became a super-hero!**

I DID IT

Off **he flew** to see the jab nurse,
HE DID IT
(With a slight lip-purse).

Fantastic Fin felt **really proud**,
he smashed that jab and cheered out loud.
Fantastic Fin the super boy wonder,
who **faced his fears** and prevailed from blunder.

Fantastic Fin went off **to bed**,
he **suddenly** was filled with dread.

His tummy was **anxious inside**,
scared of **the dark**, nowhere to hide.

Then **he thought** of something cool,
his **mind** could be a **useful** tool.

Fantastic Fin the deadly shark,
swam waters which were
really dark.

FANTASTIC FIN'S FEAR FACT FILE!

⭐ Remember that we all feel fear sometimes, it's totally normal

⭐ Facing your fears takes practise and your courage will grow over time

⭐ Don't worry if you can't always feel your courage, it's always there

⭐ Just take one step at a time

⭐ It's ok to fail, we all do

⭐ We all need help sometimes and that's ok

⭐ Close your eyes and imagine being a brave and courageous character or animal of your choice, just like I did. Close your eyes, breathe in and out and feel your courage and bravery grow within you.

⭐ Draw a picture of you facing your fears and write down what it feels like.

I'd love to see your pictures. Ask your parents to email them to me at enquiries@jessicabowers.co.uk

TIPS FOR PARENTS

⭐ The aim is to develop your child's courage to face their fears, rather than to try and 'get rid' of them. Fear is a normal and healthy feeling that we all experience.

⭐ Normalise your child's feelings of fear; they need to know that what they are experiencing is normal and understandable (even if it might not make sense to them or you).

⭐ Reassure your child that facing their fears takes practise, and it becomes easier the more they do it.

⭐ Use creative imagery like in this story to help your child embody the attributes of a courageous character or animal. Using role play and/or drawing themselves as their chosen character are great ways of developing their courage.

⭐ Talk about the qualities and attributes of courageous role models in books and films that they like.

⭐ Set small and achievable targets. If they do not achieve them, reassure them that these things can take time and that we all need help sometimes.

⭐ Make sure your child knows that it is perfectly ok to fail; failure is part of success.

⭐ Celebrate when they face their fears and demonstrate courage, no matter how small. Positive reinforcement is a great motivational tool.

⭐ Your child will be inspired by you sharing stories of when you overcame a challenge and faced your fears.

⭐ Try not to worry if you respond imperfectly, we parents get it wrong sometimes.
Try again and learn from your experience. Some of these tips have emerged from my own parenting fails.

The concept of this book was inspired by the methods I used to support my own son in facing challenges when he was a little younger — they really worked!

Jessica

ABOUT THE AUTHOR

Jessica Bowers is a Counsellor and Psychotherapist as well as a well-being writer, who is passionate about supporting and enhancing good mental health in children. She lives in Derbyshire with her lovely husband, three fab children and two tortoises!

www.jessicabowers.co.uk

📘 @jessicabowerswellbeingwriter
📷 @jessicabowerswellbeingwriter
🐦 @bowerswellbeing

ABOUT THE ILLUSTRATOR

Andrew Whitehead is an experienced illustrator of 25 years who developed a very early interest in all things artistic - since 6 to be precise.

Inspired by the vibrancy of 80s pop culture and the scribbles of Tinker Hatfield, Andrew pursued his career in illustration and now showcases appearances with worldwide enterprises such as *Arsenal*, *Yamaha*, *McDonalds*, *Pizza Express* and *Speedo*.

Clients often commission Andrew for his engaging, lively and dynamic illustrations that truly bring life to the every day. From start to finish Andrew works closely with writers and editors to ensure their vision is turned from the written word to a visual reality.

www.since6.co.uk